JANE RESH THOMAS

LIGHTS
ON THE
RIVER

ILLUSTRATED BY
MICHAEL DOOLING

Hyperion Books for Children
New York

Text © 1994 by Jane Resh Thomas.
Illustrations © 1994 by Michael Dooling.
All rights reserved.
Printed in the United States of America.
For information address Hyperion Books for Children,
114 Fifth Avenue, New York, New York 10011.

FIRST EDITION
1 3 5 7 9 10 8 6 4 2

Library of Congress Cataloging-in-Publication Data
Thomas, Jane Resh
Lights on the river/Jane Resh Thomas; illustrations
by Michael Dooling.
p. cm.
Summary: Teresa, the young daughter of Mexican-American
migrant workers, has a hard life but keeps memories of her
grandmother and Mexico alive in her heart.
ISBN 0-7868-0004-6 (trade) — ISBN 0-7868-2003-9 (lib. bdg.)
[1. Migrant labor — Fiction.   2. Mexican Americans —
Fiction.   3. Family life — Fiction.]   I. Dooling, Michael, ill.
II. Title.
PZ7.T36695Li 1994
[E] — dc20 93-33636 CIP AC

For the people who lived in the chicken coop
and all of the other workers
who labor in fields and orchards
—J.R.T.

To Dilys Evans
—M.D.

Teresa lay in the sun-flecked grass under a tree at the edge of a field. She was the baby-sitter. But while her little brother, Juan, snored softly and Aunt Luisa's baby, Julia, slept under the net that kept the bees and the flies away, Teresa could shut her eyes and listen to her family as they worked among the cucumber vines nearby.

"We've picked this field clean. The work is almost done here," said Uncle Gabriel, dropping a cucumber from each hand into a bushel basket.

"Where shall we go next?" asked Papi. "The sugar beets will be ready soon. Or the peaches." With a grunt, he picked up the full basket and carried it to the edge of the lane.

Teresa cuddled her doll, María, and watched workers all across the field stooping and rising, stooping and rising. Beyond Uncle Gabriel, Mami and Aunt Luisa looked under the vines for hidden cucumbers.

"La la la-la," they sang, "our light will light your way." And Teresa hummed with them the familiar music they sang every Christmas Eve in Mexico.

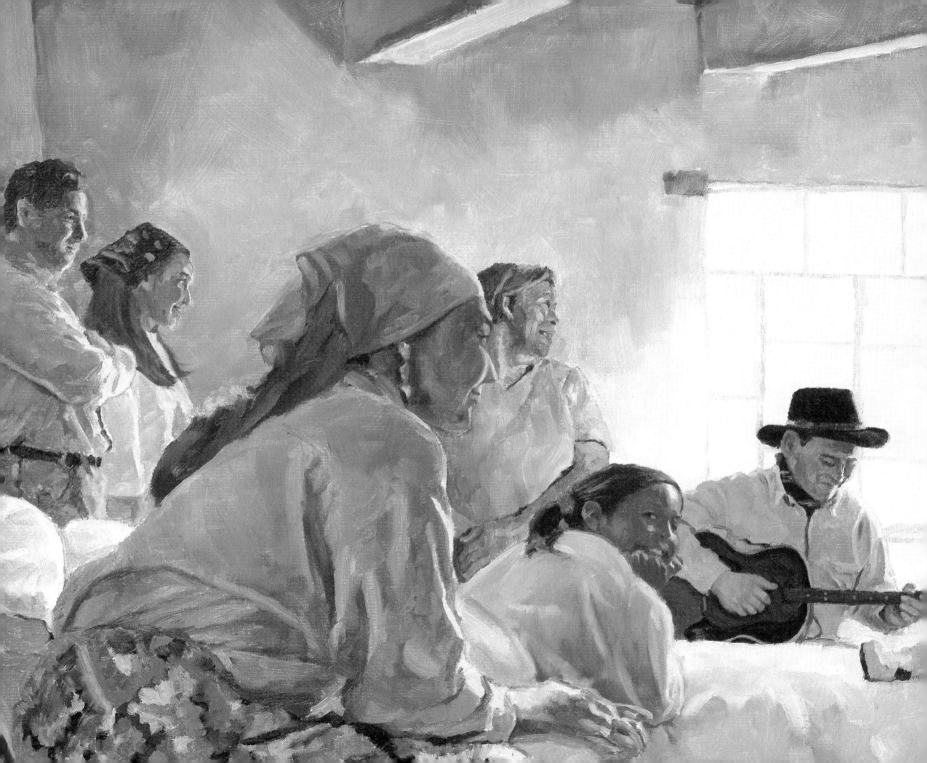

Overhead the wind shooshed in the trees, and the birds darted in and out of shadows just as they did at her grandmother's house in Mexico, far away. Teresa wished that she could fly like the birds from this hot northern field, where dust powdered everything. She would fly to Abuela, who would brush Teresa's long hair and then her own, singing all the while. On the cookstove by the door, the kettle would brim with chicken and beans and hot peppers.

Teresa's stomach growled as she remembered the food Abuela had cooked during her family's visit last Christmas. "This scrawny rooster has been scratching at the doorstep for months," Abuela had said. "I saved him for the celebration." Steam rose from the stirred pot and swirled around her head.

Abuela had raised her eyebrows and pointed at the orange-and-black oriole that sang in the tree by the window. "Teresa!" she whispered. "Listen to the music!" Papi imitated the birdsong on the highest notes of his guitar, and the family stopped talking to laugh and listen.

After dark the villagers went down the hill to the river, just as they always did on Christmas Eve. Abuela led the way because she was the oldest, while her family walked tall in the honored place behind her. One by one, everybody followed—the old people who stayed all year in the village, and the mothers and fathers with their children, home from their work in the fields. The procession wound behind Abuela on the riverbank all the way up the hill and halfway through the village.

La la la-la. Our light will light your way.

The whole village was singing the Christmas song their mothers had taught them. And everybody except the babies carried a rough wooden box sealed with wax, weighted with river sand, and lit with one burning candle.

They went to the place where the river bends. Humming together, they placed their boxes on the water, one by one. Teresa's candle floated beside Abuela's as far as they could see, streaming with the others on the soft current down the river, carrying their light to the next village, and that village's light to the next.

Three days later Teresa kissed her grandmother good-bye, saying "Abuelita," as if the whispered name would help her remember the dear face. Abuela handed Teresa a package wrapped in brown paper. "I made an extra river light for you," she said. "It is a piece of home."

Now Mexico and Christmas were far away, and Teresa tended the babies at the edge of this cucumber field. When the workers had picked the vines clean, another truck chugged up the dusky lane. Teresa watched her family and the others carry the heavy baskets across the field and hoist them onto the back of the truck.

"Peaches," said a man to Uncle Gabriel. "The peaches are ripe. This job is over, but there's work in the orchards north of here."

As she always did when the family had to move, Mami sighed. "Here in the United States we carry our house on our backs," she said. "One month, it's a cucumber farm. Another month, peaches. Then apples."

Papi touched her shoulder. "The money we earn feeds our mouths," he said gently. "And we have a little left for Abuela."

Teresa played with Juan and Julia while the tired grown-ups packed their rusty station wagon with everything they owned. First came the cooking pots and bedding and clothes, then the bags of dried beans and rice. Finally, in the safe place at the top of the pile, came Teresa's doll, María, and Papi's guitar. Beside them Mami placed Abuela's wrapped box of river sand.

The car jiggled and squeaked as it began to move through the cooling evening air. Julia screeched, and Aunt Luisa gave her milk. Whimpering, Juan sucked his thumb. Teresa leaned against the bags of clothes and fell asleep.

When she awoke, the sun was up, and a man was showing Papi an old chicken coop in a farmyard, between the road and the orchard. Rubbing her sleepy eyes, Teresa followed them up a step—really just a crate turned upside down—and into the little coop. The chickens were gone, but Teresa could still see stains on the floor where their roosts had stood. She could faintly smell the sharp ammonia memory of the flock. Somebody had poked paper into the holes in the screens; Teresa scratched her mosquito bites, imagining the whine of the swarms that would descend upon her in the night. There were no beds, just two dirty mattresses on the floor. The only other furniture was a rickety table, a chair, and two crates. An electric hot plate for cooking stood on a shelf. Papi didn't say a word.

Back in the yard, the farmer rubbed his bald head. "There's your water," he said, pointing to a hand pump in the yard. Teresa saw a dirty bar of soap in some netting and a chipped washbasin that hung from nails in a tree. She shivered, thinking of the cold baths from that basin in the twilight.

"There's the toilet." The farmer pointed to an outhouse near the barn.

She could have found the outhouse herself, Teresa thought, by following her nose. She dreaded sitting among the spiders there in the dark. Spiders didn't seem to mind bad smells.

Mami turned her back on the man, her lips a hard line as if she were swallowing loud words, and pulled Teresa into the shelter of her arm. Teresa could see Mami's anger boiling under her skin.

"We're picking today in the orchard across the road," the farmer said, "behind the school. You'll see the wagon." He climbed onto the tractor that was still running in the yard, and Teresa's family began to carry the cooking pots and bedding into the chicken coop. Teresa watched, clinging to María.

The family ate beans and tortillas for breakfast, along with some of the cucumbers they had brought from the last job. Papi and Uncle Gabriel sat on the crates. They gave Aunt Luisa the chair because she was expecting another baby; as her belly grew bigger, she groaned like an old dog when she got out of bed in the morning. Mami and Teresa stood by the table to eat, each with a baby on her hip.

Before they had finished breakfast, the woman farmer came to the door of the chicken house with a bowl of peaches and a few tomatoes, a box of eggs, and an aluminum pitcher. "Here's some milk for the children," she said.

Mami spoke English almost as well as Teresa, but this morning she refused. She handed the bowl to her daughter. The tomatoes looked so smooth, Teresa touched them with the palm of her hand. They were still warm from the sun. *"Gracias,"* said Mami.

"Never mind," said the woman. "Pretty black hair." She patted Teresa's braids, but Mami and the woman wouldn't look at one another. The farmer walked away with her head down.

Mami put the tomatoes into one of her own pots. Then she handed the bowl to Teresa. "Take it to the house," she said.

Teresa felt the fine dust squish between her toes as she walked to the farmers' back porch. Through the screen she saw the woman lift a pan from the oven. Teresa smelled a sweetness so strong she thought she could have walked on it all the way to heaven if she tried.

The woman turned when Teresa stepped on a squeaky board. She opened the door and accepted the bowl. "Want a cookie?" she said, holding out a full plate. "They're chocolate chip."

Teresa took one cookie; it was still warm. "Thank you," she whispered. But she was looking past the woman into the kitchen. Leftover breakfast sausages were still on the table, smelling fragrant and spicy. Through an inside door Teresa glimpsed a toilet under the bathroom window, where pretty curtains fluttered in the breeze. She turned and ran back to the chicken coop, devouring the cookie in one bite as she ran. Her throat was so full of anger that the cookie stuck.

While Papi slept after his long drive, the rest of Teresa's family stood on ladders, picking the peaches. All day Teresa played with the babies and gently transferred the peaches from the pickers' baskets into crates, careful not to bruise the soft fruit. Even so, juice ran down her arms, streaking the dust on her skin. Teresa watched the orioles drink from the peaches over her head, just the way the bird had pecked at the oranges in the tree outside Abuela's window on Christmas Day.

Late in the afternoon, as the babies played in the tangle of clover and purple vetch, an Anglo woman came walking up the lane.

"Buenos días," she called, greeting Mami and Aunt Luisa. And she went on speaking Spanish. "There's a concert tonight at the school by the road," she said. "You and the other farm workers are invited."

Mami answered in English. "Thank you. Perhaps we'll come, but we are very tired."

At sunset, the family walked slowly down the lane, with Juan and Julia asleep in Mami's and Aunt Luisa's arms. As they passed the Anglo school, Teresa heard a high sweet ribbon of music floating through the open door.

"*Please*, Mami," said Teresa. "The concert!"

"We are all too hungry and tired," said Mami. "Mornings in the orchard come too soon."

The music enchanted Teresa, but Uncle Gabriel took her hand and led her to the chicken coop. In the twilight, while the beans and rice simmered, while the babies slept, Teresa and her family lay on their backs in the grass, watching the stars and murmuring. Papi played a soft guitar.

The stream of Papi's music carried Teresa home again, to Mexico at Christmastime. She could see her light reflected in the water and hear the oriole sing. In her imagination, Papi and Uncle Gabriel had planted an orchard of their own. Mami ran a café with screened doors and curtains at the windows, where Teresa served beans and chicken and chocolate-chip cookies. Aunt Luisa sat at the counter, awaiting her baby's birth, and left the orchard ladders to Uncle Gabriel. Nobody's stomach growled with hunger. And every night Teresa rested in Abuela's dooryard with the people she loved, listening to Papi's guitar.

Now, in the grass by the chicken coop, Mami unwrapped Abuela's box, lit the candle, and lodged it upright in the river sand.

"But Mami," said Teresa, "the candle is for Christmas."

"We carry our house on our backs," Mami whispered in her ear, "but Abuela gave us the sand and the light to keep the village alive in our hearts."

The candle lit Mami's face. Teresa listened to Papi's song as Mami pulled her into her lap, the place that was always home.

AUTHOR'S NOTE

I wrote this story more than forty years after seeing several migrant farm workers standing at the doorstep of the chicken coop where they were housed on a Michigan farm. They might have been people whose families came from China or Nigeria, from England or Mexico; workers of every culture have labored on American farms, traveling from one place to another, picking apples or avocados or pineapples. The people I saw as a child were Mexican.

Hispanic people do every kind of work in the United States today, including service in the president's cabinet and migrant farm work. The numbers of a moving population are hard to count, but in Minnesota, my home state, some officials who assist migrant workers estimate that more than ninety percent are Hispanic. And migrant workers in Minnesota and throughout the United States are often mistreated, poorly paid, and indecently housed to this day.